How Have I Grown?

Written by Mary Reid

Illustrated by John Speirs

SCHOLASTIC INC.

New York   Toronto   London   Auckland   Sydney

For Eva,
with love and memories.
– M. R.

Library of Congress Cataloging-in-Publication Data

Reid, Mary.
How Have I Grown? / written by Mary Reid ; illustrated by John Speirs.
p. cm.
Summary: A young girl describes the ways she has changed from the time
she was a baby until she goes to kindergarten.

ISBN 0-590-49757-X
[1: Growth — Fiction.]. I. Speirs, John, ill. II. Title.
PZ7.R2727Ho 1993   93-44811
[E] — dc20

English version copyright © 1995 by Scholastic Inc.
Illustrations copyright © 1995 by Scholastic Inc.
All rights reserved. Published by Scholastic Inc.
Printed in the U.S.A.
ISBN 0-590-29298-6 (meets NASTA specifications)

36   40   22/0

I used
to be
a baby.

I slept a lot.

I cried for my food.

I splashed in my bath.

I played with my toys.

I crawled and climbed.

Then I learned to walk.

I talked and
listened
to stories.

But I was still little.
I wore diapers.
I took two naps.

I liked yogurt and applesauce
and mashed bananas.
I made a mess.

Then one day my Nana said,
"My, how you've grown!"

Then I was a little kid.

I went to preschool.
I didn't want to say goodbye.

But I could dress myself.
I had my own cubby.

I did puzzles and looked at books.

I pretended and I painted.

Sometimes I had a hard time.
I got into fights.

Sometimes I cried.
I didn't know how to share.

I ate peanut butter
and banana
sandwiches.

I rode a tricycle.
I went up the climber.

My daddy said, "My, how you've grown!"

Now I'm a big kid!

I'm in kindergarten!

I am taller.

My feet are
bigger.

My old jacket
is too small.

I can build
with blocks.

I can count to ten.

I can write my name,
and other words, too.

I can measure and compare.

I can help take care of Bunty.

I can make up stories!

I can listen to my friends tell stories, too.

I can comfort my friend.

I can take turns and share.

My, how I've grown!